My Poopie Puppy

First print edition February 2016

Book design by Joshua McManus

Published by Imaginary Publishing
www.imaginarypublishing.com

PLOP!

I brought myself a puppy, he was money well spent.
I was very excited and off home we went.

My puppy seemed happy as he walked through the door,
He jumped, barked and rolled on the floor.

But he had the weirdest look on his face
And pooped all over the fireplace.

But I didn't get angry, not the slightest bit mad;
He was my new friend, so he shouldn't feel sad.

To the bath he went, and I scrubbed his back end,
I do love my puppy, my lovely new friend.

So after some time in lovely warm bath,
He jumped in garden and ran up the path.

But just like before, that look on his face.
Oh no! he's pooping all over the place!

He pooped on bench and over the wall,
with so much poop for a puppy so small!

So, I quickly called him, and he walked right in.
But he carried on pooping right in my bin.

He pooped on the table and on the chair.
He pooped in my slippers – a brand new pair.

And if there is one thing I just can't bear,
It's a puppy pooping everywhere.

So I took him to the vet to find out what was wrong.
The vet said try a dog calming song.

Well, that didn't work. He didn't stop.
He pooped all over the vet's clean top.

"Your dog is still a puppy and that's what puppies do,
So, prepare, and be ready to clean up lots of poo."

So we left the vet's and back home we came,
The house was dirty and no longer the same.

But my puppy had a smile on his face.
And pooped right off my lovely bookcase.

That pop flew through the air and then hit the telly,
A yucky poop, so very smelly.

He pooped on the sofa and on the rug.
He pooped up high, knocked over a jug.

Maybe the idea of getting a puppy was so very bad;
This day is by far the worst I've had.

A tear rolled from my eye,
I was just about to cry.

But PING! A thought came into my head.
Why hadn't I thought of this instead?

So I rummaged through my drawers to find it.
It was soft, white and the perfect fit.

But what is my idea I bet you can't guess.
It will stop this puppy's awful mess.

Finally I could say goodbye to all that smelly
puppy poop, at last I was so happy.

And all I did was put him in an extra soft white nappy.

Read more by
Joshua McManus

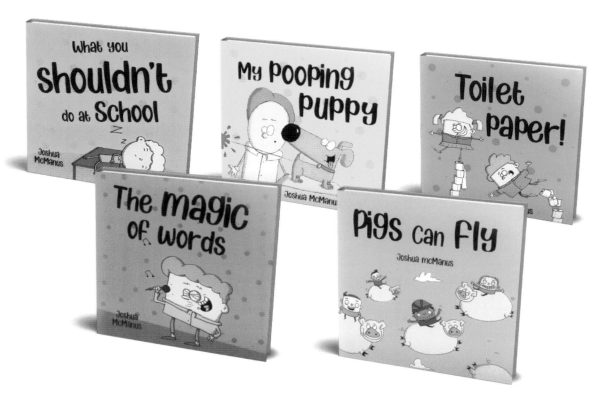

Printed in Great Britain
by Amazon